Free Play RPG

Expansion II

By
Donte Alarcon

ISBN: 9798738958199

Cover design by: Art Painter
Printed in the United States of America

CONTENT

FREE PLAY RPG

INTRODUCTION

Welcome back! Hopefully by this time you have had a chance to learn the basics of the system and have had a chance to play a few games with your friends. The idea of the Free Play RPG system was designed to be easy to learn so that the Game Master (GM) and players could just jump right in and play. This expansion makes this process even easier by getting you started with a lot of the basics so that you can start up your games faster or even help build your imagination to give you that head start into building your own world, weapons, and general structure to bring your game to life.

Expansion II is meant to make the task of the GM a bit easier. If you are the GM, this expansion will help you with world building and creating NPCs (non player characters) to populate your world. This expansion will also show you how to create unique weapons which will enhance your gameplay and add a new level of depth to how your players choose their arsenal.

In addition, this book will expand on the Hero Expansion from the first book. There will be a section on creating powered weapons (weapons that have powers attached to them) and a section that breaks down the various superhero archetypes which should help to make it easier for players to build their own characters as well as the GM building super powered NPCs.

WORLD BUILDING

In this section we go over world building. What is world building you ask? It is basically creating all the elements that make up the world the players will be a part of. It is in the best interest of creating the "story" that background elements of the world are created even if the players will never encounter them. This adds depth to the world and gives a level of weight to how the players make decisions. An example of this is if you are playing a setting like the Wild Wild West. If you shoot somebody in a public space, maybe there will be little alarm to your actions. On the flip side if you shoot somebody in an open public area in a modern time setting, you run the risk of alarming the public and having the authorities after you. In addition, building the unseen parts of your world makes it easier to prepare if the players decide to change up from what you originally intended for them to do.

So the first part of world building is coming up with the time frame and the setting. After that you will need to define the "climate" of the world. This means the sum total of the way things work like politics, the state of mind of the general public, the law of the world, and so on. The time frame is simply the year if it is in a setting within our normal world. In the normal world, the time frame along with the setting (location) will give you the climate of the world or area automatically. In fictional worlds, you may have to define the time, setting, and the climate separately. Maybe you want to play in a post apocalyptic setting which is 100 years into the future of the modern day. Or maybe you want to play in a fantasy setting with knights, kings and dragons which takes place many years in the past (and of course not our normal past). So take the time to figure out where and when you want things to take place.

3

The climate of the world can play a large part in how the world is populated. If you were playing a dystopian future world, is it safe to walk outside? Will you be hunted? If you are playing a heroes game, are people with powers force to be in hiding because the world no longer accepts them? Maybe this world is run by a rich and powerful company that runs the last modern city while everything else around it is desert land. This is for you to decide. Here we will focus on creating elements that help with a normal modern setting but feel free to modify anything to fit a setting that is more to your liking.

A key factor in building your world is populating it. The easiest way to do this is to start with the generic characters that populate your world. Here we will list a few stats for basic archetypes. From here, this will allow you to throw somebody into a situation like a random person passing by and already have stats to just pull out and use for them. Feel free to modify any stats at any point in time to suit your game.

General NPCs

Civilian
Strength - 1
Fighting - 2
Agility - 2
Accuracy - 2
Health - 15

Cop
Strength - 2
Fighting - 5
Agility - 6
Accuracy - 7
Health - 17

Weapons:
Handgun (d12)
Bulletproof Vest (10 health)

Thug
Strength - 2
Fighting - 4
Agility - 4
Accuracy - 3
Health - 17

Weapon:
Knife (d6)
Handgun (d12)

Soldier
Strength - 3
Fighting - 9
Agility - 6
Accuracy - 12
Health - 18

Weapons:
Flak Jacket (15 Health)
Knife (d6)
Handgun (d12)
Rifle (d12 + d4)

Ninja
Strength - 2
Fighting - 10
Agility - 10
Accuracy - 9
Health - 18

Weapons:
Katana Sword (d8)
Throwing Knives (d6)

Settings

Listed below are some alternative setting suggestions to help you with your world building.

Post Apocalyptic
Time: Future
Setting Climate:
Wasteland like with very little civil society left. A few small cities exist with towering skyscrapers which have great walls surrounding them protecting them from the outside world. The cities are primarily occupied by the wealthy while some working level population exist in the cities to keep things running. The outside world is dangerous and harsh. People scavenge the land and even hunt others for what little they may have.

Utopia
Time: Future
Setting Climate:
Paradise of modern technology and healthy living. Civil order is at an all time high and there is little crime. The smallest offenses are not taken lightly. But below the eyes of the public is a shady underworld. High level crime bosses in high level positions in society use their power to gain more power and are in touch with the black market and lower level street criminals. Criminals function either in the cyber world or in underground hidden cities where the law does not reach. Normal society does not know of the underhanded deeds that take place in this world and all looks normal and peaceful on the surface.

Fantasy
Time: Ancient times
Setting Climate:

This is your basic fantasy realm with fantasy creatures. Elves, ogres, orcs and dragons. Choose the political or social dynamics that best fits the story/world you are trying to create.

Space
Time: Future
Setting Climate:

Far far into the future life exist primarily in space. Large spaceships are used as cities. There is a very developed political system which keeps order thru a heavily military based government system. Choose whether this world is occupied by alien species.

Modern Heroes
Time: Modern
Setting Climate:

This takes place in modern times with superheroes being a major part of the world. You have many heroes with secret identities who are unknown while you also have a few iconic heroes who are publicly known and viewed as champions of a particular area (or the world). In this setting it is also known that criminals can be super as well. This setting can potentially be the largest depending on how much you want to develop it. You can create a list of supporting heroes and villains that make up the world. You can also create other dimensions, other nations (like underwater civilizations or hidden islands of a particular group of people) and even god like beings who rule over how the universe operates. It is suggested that if you plan on using this setting as your main setting you return to for future games, you can take your time building this setting up to be its own living world with no limit to the scope of what makes it up.

Golden Age Heroes

Time: 1940-1970

Setting Climate:

This is basically similar to the Modern Heroes setting but the scale will be much smaller and focused on a particular area or time period that reflects that golden age. Maybe you have just a handful of heroes that are known but almost all are in the spotlight and are all considered clearly good guys (and not anti-heroes). The villains are clearly defined as villains though most will not be too dark in their nature. Also it is fitting for this time frame that the heroes are not overly powerful. The power of the heroes seem to go hand and hand with the level of technology for the most part (older technology and weaker heroes) so that heroes do not come off as being overpowered against your everyday criminal. It is also suggested you limit the power class levels of your players in this setting.

Hero Level of Settings

Within each setting in which you are playing as superheroes, a starting level is determined by the GM. This does not only reflect the amount of building points the players start off with, but also the caps the players have on their abilities. Each hero level has a name and set of details that go along with it.

Street Level

Street level hero is how it sounds. A hero designed for basic street level threats. These heroes are often just normal humans with some skills and/or equipment. This level can also represent very low level superpowered beings. Such superpowered beings might have a singular power with physical stats that would not exceed slightly above human levels. Typically this type of encounter will have you against street gangs, corrupt business empires and criminal empires.

Suggested power levels are as follows: Class 3 maximum for offensive powers. Rarely would anybody at this level have reality and time manipulation powers.

Mid Superhuman Level

Mid superhuman level is a setting in which heroes take on threats greater than that of a city area limit. These heroes can be quite powerful but often not unstoppable by normal threats in large quantities. This type of encounter would have you against other mid level super beings or even group entities with military level weapons.

Suggested power levels are as follows: Class 5 maximum for offensive powers.

High Superhuman Level

High superhuman level is where the heroes are globally known to solve all earthly problems. They handle threats that would otherwise threaten nations and even the world itself. The extent of power these heroes possess make them far beyond the level of the most powerful military weapons. This type of encounter would have you against other high level super beings or even cosmic threats if you are a large group.

Suggested power levels are as follows: Class 7 maximum offensive powers.

Cosmic Level

Cosmic level is how it sounds. A hero designed for stopping threats that are beyond earth. These heroes usually cover the span of galaxies and protect entire worlds. The powers of cosmic powered beings are limitless and they can range from being basic to being able to do anything they can imagine. This type of encounter would have you saving entire worlds from threats that can literally destroy planets.

No suggested power limits.

Note: These suggested levels are only a guide to help structure your game play and are not required.

WEAPONS

Weapons makeup an important part of the game. Weapons can help you out when you are in a jam. The core book went over the basics of weapons. In this section we are going to give greater detail to the weapons which will add more depth to your game in the way players select their weapons. This chapter will be broken down into sections explaining firearms, other weapons and equipment.

Firearms

In the real world, not all firearms are the same and not all ammo or magazines are compatible with all types of firearms. Firearms usually come with their own magazines design for that specific firearm. The magazine is simply a container to hold the ammo used for that firearm. Though many guns will support the same type of ammo, if that ammo is loaded in a specific magazine for one type of firearm, you would not be able to use that ammo unless you take each bullet out of the one magazine and load it into the magazine of the gun you are using. The reason this is important is because it is important to know when you are in-game and in a tight situation where your gun runs out of ammo, you cannot just pick up the magazine to the guy you may have just killed and put it in your gun and just go about your way.

Below will be listed a set of made-up firearms for this in-game world that have specific details about them. Feel free to create your own or use real world firearms and give them specific details matching how they

11

function in the real world. Refer to the core book for the rules on how firearms work.

MP Cult - (d12 + d4) (+2 Accuracy) The MP Cult is a machine gun that comes in all black finishing. The MP Cult comes standard with a scope attached (increasing the accuracy). The MP Cult supports full auto and semi auto (2 shots per attack or 1 shot per attack. Must declare before making the attack). The magazine size is 30 rounds. This gun can support a red dot aim.

This is the gold standard for professionals. It is quite expensive, even on the black market, so you will almost never find it in the hands of criminals. This high quality firearm comes standard with many higher end features and tends to never jam.

MP Crew - (d12 + d4) The MP Crew is a machine gun that comes in all black finishing. The MP Crew only supports full auto (2 shots per attack). The magazine size is 20 rounds. This gun is not capable of supporting a scope. This gun can support a red dot aim.

The cheaper cousin to the MP Cult, the MP Crew is never used by professionals (like military or law enforcement) but often used by criminals. It is cheap to make and so it is sold for much less than the MP Cult making it high damage for a bargain. It tends to have jamming problems and has a relatively low magazine capacity for this type of gun.

MP Club - (d12 + d4) The MP Club is a heavy machine gun that comes in all black finishing. The MP Club supports full auto and semi auto (2 shots per attack or 1 shot per attack. Must declare before making the attack). The magazine size is 40 rounds and only takes heavy A.P.R. bullets (+2 damage). This gun can support a scope and red dot aim attachment. (Operates with magnum rules for the dice rolls)

Strictly for military use only, the MP Club brings the party. It is the larger, heavier version of the MP Cult designed for doing serious damage. Forget price, this weapon is not permitted in the hands of civilians at all. The MP Club will almost never find its way onto the black market.

Wingman/Sidekick - (d12) Both of these are 9mm guns that share the same specifications other than the Wingman is silver in color while the Sidekick is black in color. Both have interchangeable magazines. They fit either a 10 round or 15 round magazine size. Both can support a red dot aim.

Both of these guns are considered the standard for a handgun. They rarely jam and are equally used by criminals and professional a like.

HH - (d12) The HH (Helping Hand) is a 9mm style magnum. The body is silver in color with a black color handle grip and is larger than your standard Wingman or Sidekick. The HH magnum can fit either a 10 round or 15 round magazine but only takes heavy A.P.R. bullets (+2 damage). This gun can support a scope.

The HH is the gun everybody wants but not everybody can get. It will stop a person instantly. Though they can be found on the black market, they are rare and they fetch a very high price. Sometimes they are also used for hunting but have strict requirements to qualify to purchase one.

Showstopper - (d12 + d4) The Showstopper is a black barrel, wooden handle shotgun. The Showstopper has an external magazine that holds 10 rounds (compared to some shotguns that have an internal magazine and load the ammo straight into the gun). The Showstopper does not support a red dot aim but does support a scope.

The Showstopper is a fan favorite of shotgun users because of its relatively large ammo capacity vs traditional shotguns and the fact that it can reload quick using its external magazine vs internal magazine which takes much longer to load and usually has a limited capacity of about 5 to 6 bullets.

Spindle - (d12) The Spindle is a revolver gun. It is silver in color and has black wooden accents on the handle. It holds 6 rounds and requires a full action to reload. The Spindle can support a scope.

The Spindle was a classic gun used for law enforcement back in the days. Now it is mostly owned by collects. Criminals often still use it because it is very cheap and easy to get a hold of. Never bring a Spindle to a Sidekick fight.

Whirlwind - (d12) The Whirlwind is a revolver style magnum. The Whirlwind has a long muzzle and is silver in color and has brown wooden accents on the handle. It holds 6 rounds and only takes heavy A.P.R. bullets. It requires a full action to reload. The Whirlwind can support a scope.

The classic "take no crap" gun of legend. Though it is dated, it is still hard to get a hold off because they are in short supply. The power it possesses still makes it a viable option today even though it has low ammo capacity compared to a 9mm.

Fiska Rifle - (d12 + d4) The Fiska rifle is all black in color with a wooden handle. The Fiska has an internal magazine and holds 5 rounds. Ammo is loaded straight into the gun and requires a full action to reload. The Fiska supports a red dot aim and scope.

The Fiska is very popular. It is used for hunting usually though some civilians use it for basic home protection. It is considered a great cheap option because it can be upgraded easily. Its only major weakness when it comes to combat is its slow reload rate and low ammo capacity.

Slowstopper - (d12 + d4) The Slowstopper is a gun metal gray, wooden handle shotgun. The Showstopper has an internal magazine that holds 6 rounds. Ammo is loaded straight into the gun and requires a full action to reload. The Slowstopper does not support a red dot aim but does support a scope.

The Slowstopper is your run of the mill shotgun. It is very popular in home defense for normal civilians or store owners. Criminals will also run to it as a means of heavy firepower because it has less requirements to purchase one. It is affordable and does not raise any red flags for purchase.

Stinger - (d10) The Stinger is a very small gun, palm size. Gun metal body color, wooden handle side accent. It only holds 5 rounds in an internal magazine. The Stinger does not support gun attachments.

The Stinger is one of the smallest guns around. It is commonly used to be snuck around for assassination jobs in which you need to get a gun into tight areas. The only issue is the power it punches is so weak, you are just as likely to use a knife and have better results.

Wildflower (Plus) - (d20 + 5) The Wildflower and Wildflower Plus is an all black finish grenade launcher. The standard holds 6 rounds while the Plus holds 8 rounds. Unlike a standard grenade, the rounds in a grenade launcher are more like large bullets (so you cannot use them by hand). The Wildflower does not support a scope or a red dot aim.

Only used by military, this weapon is illegal for all other uses. On the black market the Wildflower is extremely expensive and the Plus is very hard to come by and even more expensive. Criminals pay top dollar for these because they can make short work of any problem.

Mini Wild - (d20 + 5) The Mini Wild is a grenade launcher attachment that fits on the front of most machine guns. The Mini Wild holds 3 rounds.

The Mini Wild is the easiest and most affordable way to get your hands on a grenade launcher. That is not to say it is cheap. Normally only for military use but it has recently flooded the black market.

Other Weapons

There are many different weapons that do not fall into the simple categories mentioned in the core book. Listed here will be weapons you may not have thought of and how they differ from some of their similar counterparts. Some weapons that will be listed are a common staple of superheroes.

Throwing Knives - (d6) The difference between throwing knives vs regular knives are that they are particularly designed for throwing and are usually not very durable for hand-to-hand combat (though they can be used this way). Throwing knives have the benefit of being very slim and small in length so 5 of them can take up the same space as 1 standard knife would in your storage pack. Shurikens (Ninja stars) count as the same thing.

Throwing knives or shurikens usually have a one time use life span as they tend to damage once they hit their target.

Modern Compound Bow - (d10) This type of bow shoots further than a standard traditional bow. Some versions of this type of bow can support a scope and red dot aim.

These type of bows can be very expensive but most professionals prefer to use these in competitions or in hunting because they shoot a lot further and can be far more accurate vs traditional bows because of the attachments.

Special Arrows - Arrows can be customized for different effects. A few special arrows will be listed below. Standard quiver size is 24 arrows and the large quiver size is 32 arrows.

- Explosive Arrows: (d20 + 5) (Explosion) Refer to the core book on rules for explosion. *Not cheap to produce but is the most effective arrow for causing damage.*

- Poison Arrows: (d4/60%) (d8/60%) (d8/90%) Refer to the rules on poison in the core book. *The stronger the poison, the more the arrow cost to make.*

- Cryo Arrow: (d10) Target becomes frozen. Refer to the rules on freeze power in the core book. *Usually quite expensive to produce but can be quite effective at slowing somebody down or even freezing a doorway behind you for a quick getaway.*

- Snare Arrow: (2 damage) Target is stuck in a hold. Refer to the rules on webs in the core book. *These type of arrows are pretty cheap to make and great for trapping a target.*

- Armor Piercing Arrows (light and heavy): (+1 or +2 damage to the base damage) *Armor piercing arrows can be very expensive to produce but are extremely dangerous.*

- Grapple Arrow: This grappling hook arrow is used for climbing, swinging, and getting to hard to reach places. *These arrows are not designed for attack and simply used as a means of travel so they are very affordable to make lots of them.*

Bo Staff - (d8) The bo staff is a pretty basic martial weapon. In recent years it has been highly adopted by superheroes. A subcategory of the bo staff is the custom bo staff. Some examples of the custom bo staff:
- Breakaway Bo: Starts as a whole staff (d8) but breaks apart into 2 smaller separate batons (d6).

- Grapple Bo: This bo staff has a breakaway tip that can shoot off a grappling hook of 50ft long.

The standard bo staff is a very inexpensive weapon in general though the price can increased based on the material and durability. The custom bo staff, depending on the design and added features, can be very expensive. But before you can consider price, you would be hard press to find somebody who has the skill to do such custom work.

Metal Knuckles - (d6) A simple tool to add a bit of extra damage to your punches. Metal knuckles are great for an easy to conceal weapon.

A cheap and easy weapon to come by but it is considered illegal in some states.

Standard Shield - (d6) A standard shield is your basic shield held in your hand or mounted on your arm to protect against attacks like the days of old. Though it can be used to hit somebody with, its primary function is defense. A shield is meant to absorb some of the damage from the attacks that come your way. It works similar to some armored suits that provide damage resistance. The difference is while an armor suit with damage resistance has a health stat, a shield will have a maximum hit stat. This stat indicates how many hits (not damage value) the shield can take before it breaks. A wood shield provides resistance 1 (Energy, Physical) damage with a maximum hit value of 5 while a steel shield provides resistance 3 (Energy, Physical) damage with a maximum hit value of 10.

- Wood Shield: R - 1 (E,P) 5 Hits.
- Steel Shield: R - 3 (E,P) 10 Hits.

A shield is a great way to have damage resistance at a relatively low cost. It is not the most convenient option for some situations and sometimes looks out of place in modern times, but things like that do not matter for heroes. You will never see this item in a conventional setting but there always seems to be at least one hero sporting one on a team.

*If a wood shield is hit 5 times (or a steel shield 10 times), regardless of the damage done, it will be destroyed. Example; if you take 10 points of damage and you have a steel shield, you will receive 7 points of damage to your hero and the shield will only be able to take 9 more attacks before it is destroyed. Shields do not stack with other resistance. Use the highest source of damage resistance you have access to.

*If you want an indestructible shield for your hero, you can pay for a shield with your power points to build the shield manually (costing the price of damage resistance) and adding the feature; unbreakable. This would fall under a power weapon even if it is not mystical in origin.

Equipment

Just as important to somebody on a mission as their weapons is their equipment. Equipment is probably more important to saving your life than your offensive weapons. Sometimes having a means to escape conflict, avoid it, or heal from it is the key to survival. Listed below will be some basic equipment along with some special equipment occasionally used by superheroes.

Binoculars - Basic tool for seeing long distance.

Many superheroes like to carry a pair of these for espionage or simply to make up for not having enhanced vision powers.

Grappling Hook - This has two forms, traditional and mechanical. Traditional is a hook attached to the end of a rope. Mechanical is a small device a little larger than a handgun that houses a hook or claw-like metal tip with coiled wire (50ft) in the handle of the device. The mechanical grappling hook shoots out under pressure and has a mechanism to retract pulling the user towards the desired destination.

The traditional grappling hook is obviously very cheap and easy to purchase but is not very fast or sophisticated in its execution. The mechanical grappling hook has many advantages over the traditional but can be very expensive.

Body Armor - Body armor is pretty much the same as a flak jacket but it is woven or formatted into a suit (dress suit, superhero suit, etc). +10 or 15 Health (non healable). Usually thinner armor (+10) is placed in dress suits as to be undetectable while thicker armor (+15) is placed in superhero suits or tactical gear.

Body armor can be expensive but it can make the difference between living or dying. Some hitmen or personal security who wear dress/business suits align it with body armor on the inside. Superheroes who are human usually align their suits with body armor to make up for not having superhuman durability.

Utility Belt - Ideal for storing small items. Holds up to 10 pouches on the belt which can fit small size items in each pouch (cellphone, single folding knife, 5 throwing knives, 5 sticky gauze, 3 suture kits, small binoculars, metal knuckles, etc). *Can use same specifications for a tactical vest.

Usually used by officials or law enforcement (including military), this is an essential go to for superheroes who need to carry light.

Backpack - Basic storage for holding items on the go. Usually can fit several hand size items. Refer to the GM for specifics but usually about 8 hand size items can fit in the backpack.

There is nothing special about this item and it is the cheapest way to hold items on your person.

POWER WEAPONS

Sometimes superheroes rely on more than just their own powers. In some cases superheroes have powerful weapons that either aid them or are their source of power altogether. In this section we are going to go over the creation of power weapons. These are weapons that you use your power points to create when playing a super powered game.

Now power weapons are primarily for flavor but they do have some small benefits beyond just spicing up the game and making your character cool. The cost to attach your powers to a basic weapon/item is free. So though you have the negative of that your powers are not attached to you, you have the benefit of a slightly better offense if your powers are attached to an offensive weapon. There are positives to attaching your powers to basic items as well (like a ring or medallion). In this case when you attach your powers to a basic item, they can be hidden easily (like walking into a place were no weapons are allowed) and even passed along to a friend so they can use the powers.

Now if you choose to create a power weapon, this does not mean you need to place all your powers into a weapon/item. Maybe you might choose to make all your physical enhancements part of your base powers while you have a sword or an axe that can shoot energy blast and grants the user teleport. The same basic rules for applying powers to your character are the same for applying to your weapon/item. Feel free to also add a feature power to make your weapon return on command or indestructible as added security. Though usually it is assumed though that the GM's objective should not be to take the player's weapon away or make the player lose their weapon permanently as that would be no fun to the player.

Listed below will be a few examples of power weapons/items to help players or GMs create characters with weapons that might compliment their style or image.

Basic Breakdown

1) Name your weapon/item. You may choose to place the type of weapon/item in the name (so you know what it is) or next to the name in parenthesis. Also feel free to write a description of the weapon/item if it requires it.

2) Next to the weapon, place its normal damage value. Items do not have a damage value.

3) Place a dash below the weapon/item listing each power attached to the weapon/item.

Axe of Gaia (d8)
- (+25 tons) strength damage.
- Earth (solid) Blast (up to 3 targets) and control (d20 + d8 + 10)
- Healing (d12)
- Energy Healing (up to 3 targets) (d12)
- Feature: Indestructible

For the first power, strength power is purchased to add to the damage of the weapon. This means only for the use of attacking with this weapon, you add your base strength and add the strength of the weapon and then roll a d8 for your total damage. Refer to the core rule book in the powers section for adding multiple strength bonuses and calculating a total.

The next power is an energy (elemental, solid) blast and control. So this weapon gets an energy stat. This weapon also is able to blast up to 3 targets in one attack or affect 3 targets with its elemental control. The force of the elemental control is also dictated by the energy stat (whether used for attacking a subject or the amount of force used when manipulating something thru the elemental control power). Refer to the core rule book on energy in the power section.

The next power of this axe is that it grants the user healing of d12 at the beginning of their turn. Healing (vs energy/magic healing) is a free action. This power is followed by energy healing which requires an action regardless if it is used on yourself or others. The energy healing of this axe can heal up to 3 targets total (if you choose to heal yourself, it counts as one of the targets). With energy/magic healing, the user can use all of their actions to heal which would equal a total of d12 three times to 3 targets.

The final power is a feature which makes the axe indestructible. Though you would hope your GM would not try to ever destroy your weapons/items, this adds a bit of security.

This would be consider an advance build because unlike a weapon/item with one ability attached to it, this weapon has several powers.

Power Weapon/Item Examples and Tips

Ring of Strength - 100 tons of strength.

Stone of Protection - Energy Shield (d20 + d8)

Though this item provides an energy shield for defense, it has a class 5 energy stat. The user is consider to have an energy stat as if they purchased the energy power but only chose shield. If there is ever a situation where the GM says another power can be used or something requires the use of an energy source, this item would count as an energy source. Example would be if an outside source provided the power of wish/reality manipulation (which is directly enhanced by an energy stat).

Though powers cannot be used on others (like using your shield to defend somebody else), you can attach powers to items and give those items to other players. An example would be one player passing along Ring of Strength or Stone of Protection (or both) to another player in which they could use. If you wanted to play a support character, you could do so strictly based on the powers you posses like energy/magic healing but if you want to take it a step further you can have support power items which you can give before a dangerous encounter.

Boots of the Swift - Run speed 770mph
- Feature: Run on walls.

The Never Touch (Magical Body Armor)
- 100 Health
- Healing (d4)
- R - 2 (E,P)

In the case of armor, things like health, healing or resistance is for the armor and not the user underneath. When the armor reaches zero health, it can no longer heal itself. It can no longer be used and the user will not gain the benefits until returning to their base of operations (usually after finishing an event sequence) to repair the armor (whether it is mechanical or magic based). Armor normally does not absorb the damage of mind attacks and mind attacks will go straight to the health of the user underneath, but you can pay for the feature power to allow armor to absorb mind attacks. Adding such a feature would make mind attacks affect the base health of the armor instead of the user underneath.

Third Eye of All Sight (small circular item)
- Super Sense (Sight only)
- X-ray Vision
- True Sight
- Precognition (2 ranks)

This item stacks the powers of X-ray vision and true sight with super sense allowing them to work at super distances.

HERO ARCHETYPES

  Making your character is one of the funnest parts of the game but turning them into a super character is even more fun! This is not always an easy task as it can become overwhelming deciding how you want your super character to be. In this chapter we go over the different kinds of general archetypes of heroes. Not every hero fits into an archetype but most do and this will make it a bit easier in helping you decide how you want to design your hero.

  Archetypes will be listed below with some having sub-categories and all will have a brief explanation of the type and how they are best used or their role in the world or on a team. Not all archetypes are built equally and some may cater more to different types of play. Let's go over the many different hero archetypes listed here.

Paragon

Paragons are your typical heroes hero. Sometimes paragon archetypes seem more like an ideal instead of a built type. They almost always represent the symbol of good and fairness. But they do come in a common build type. Such is the caped paragon, non-caped paragon and the soldier just to name a few.

Your caped paragon is your most common type of paragon which usually is sporting the typical array of powers such as super strength, super durability, flight and a variety of utility powers.

Example Stats:
Caped Paragon
Description: (Describe how your character looks)
Strength - 38
Fighting - 7
Agility - 7
Accuracy - 8
Health - 300

Powers:
Lift - 100 tons
Flight - 10 mps
Super Senses
X-ray vision
Heal - d4
P/T - Immune
R - 4 (E, P)

The non-caped paragon is a bit more simplified usually only having super strength and super durability. The non-caped paragon may have small additional abilities like being able to jump a few hundred feet or run a bit faster than a normal man, but in general does not have crazy or extreme additional abilities. The non-caped paragon has a lot in common with your typical brick build but is never monstrous.

Example Stats:
Non-Caped Paragon
Description: (Describe how your character looks)
Strength - 31
Fighting - 10
Agility - 8
Accuracy - 8
Health - 300

Powers:
Lift - 70.9 tons
Leap - 100ft
Run - 60mph
Heal - d4
P/T - 60
R - 3 (E, P)

Last in this list is the soldier. The soldier paragon is often only slightly above human levels but still symbolizes the same ideals as your other paragons. The soldier paragon will usually try to make up in his shortcomings by training very hard and usually keeps a key weapon by his side at all times.

Example Stats:
Soldier Paragon
Description: (Describe how your character looks)
Strength - 8
Fighting - 18
Agility - 15
Accuracy - 14

Health - 25

Powers:
Lift - 800lbs
Heal - d4
P/T - 60

Weapons:
Sledge Hammer of Justice (d8)

The soldier build may appear not much more than your average crime fighter build but is actually a lot more powerful in actual play. In a street level game the soldier can actually take on 2 or 3 regular guys at once (though not if they are heavily armed). You can choose to arm the soldier build with guns as well but his physical build is more than enough to take on your average guy with a gun.

Crime Fighter/Vigilante

The crime fighter and the vigilante make up the primary bulk of your street level heroes. They usually consist of a normal human who is either trained very well or may have some pretty good equipment to aid him in his missions. The difference between the crime fighter vs the vigilante is that the crime fighter often is just trying to help people and make society a bit more safer for the average citizen while the vigilante may be a little crazy and thinks he is the only answer to solving the crime problems that have taken over his city and often in an extreme manner. Three common build types for this archetype is the masked crime fighter/vigilante, gun toting crime fighter/vigilante and the archer type (crime fighter/vigilante).

Unlike the movies, this level of character (street level) in the game is a bit more grounded in reality. This means you will not be able to walk into a room of 20 guys and beat them all up with just your fist. The average guy is nearly equal to yourself and at best maybe you can take on 2 men at once and will probably come out of the battle very badly injured. You will rely heavily on your body armor (usually built into your suit/costume) and first aid while out in the field. Try to take on enemies one at a time if possible and assess your situation after each battle.

The masked type primarily uses gadgets for his arsenal. Half of his gadgets are utility type equipment which really helps him in a pinch. The masked type focuses on hand-to-hand skills as well as a balance of offensive and defensive weapons/equipment.

Example Stats:
Masked Crime Fighter/Vigilante
Description: (Describe how your character looks. Describe the costume worn including things like utility belt or how you hold your weapons.)
Strength - 3
Fighting - 15

Agility - 12
Accuracy - 12
Health - 20

Powers:
Defensive Fighting

Weapons:
Body Armor +15 health (not healable)
Throwing knives x10 (d6)
Hand bomb x3 (d20+5)
Sticky Gauze x3
Suture kit
Expandable Bo Staff (d8)

With the masked build, you want to focus on being stealthy and not trying to be seen. Avoiding the fight is important as the masked hero does not have the offense to compete with large numbers. Of course you will have a few emergency items up your sleeves like hand thrown explosives but these should be saved for when you have no other options. A common weapon/equipment layout for the masked hero is a utility belt with throwing knives, hand explosives, grappling hook, first aid, and a melee weapon like a staff or standard knives.

The gun toter focuses on the use of heavy firepower. He will usually be equipped with several guns on his person and as much ammo as he can carry without slowing him down. Sometimes the gun toter will even stash extra firepower hidden in a bag near his mission site just in case. This build is obviously about offense and very little in the way of defense or utility.

Example Stats:
Gun Toting Crime Fighter/Vigilante

Description: (Describe how your character looks. Describe the costume worn including things like utility belt or how you hold your weapons.)
Strength - 3
Fighting - 12
Agility - 9
Accuracy - 18
Health - 20

Powers:
Defensive Fighting

Weapons:
Flak Jacket +15 health
MP Cult (w/scope) (d12+d4)
MP Cult magazine (30)x2
Sidekick (d12)
Combat Knife (d6)
Grenades x3 (d20+5)
Sticky Gauze x3

The gun toting hero often has the firepower to take on a few guys at once (depending on what they are armed with) but from a distance. Once the enemy gets close to you, things change and become more of a danger. With the gun toting hero you must always be aware of your ammo thru out your mission. Typically this hero will have a layout of one machine gun, a handgun, grenades, and a knife.

The archer type is exactly as it sounds. He uses a bow as his main weapon of choice. This is not a practical weapon but it makes up for its shortcomings with style and special arrows. The archer focuses on accuracy and has more offense than defense in his equipment setup (usually).

Example Stats:
Archer Crime Fighter/Vigilante
Description: (Describe how your character looks. Describe the costume worn including things like utility belt or how you hold your weapons.)
Strength - 3
Fighting - 10
Agility - 10
Accuracy - 19
Health - 20

Powers:
Defensive Fighting

Weapons:
Body Armor +15 health
Sticky Gauze x3
Baton (d8) x2
Modern Compound Bow w/scope
Quiver (32)
-Regular Arrows (d10) x20
-Explosive Arrows (d20+5) x3
-Armor Piercing Arrows (d10+2) x5
-Cryo Arrows (d10) x3
-Grapple Arrow

With the archer, you are playing at a disadvantage in your standard attacks (normal arrows vs a gun). But you will have access to special arrows which you just cannot have with a gun. Save your special arrows for the appropriate situation as you will not have many of them. For the archer it is very important to also have a melee weapon because you will probably run out of arrows way before your mission is over. Try to save your arrows for when you have distance on your side.

If you want to give your crime fighter/vigilante build a slight edge beyond normal human, feel free to give them a utility power. Such examples could include super senses, radar/six sense, probability control/ luck, or healing.

Warrior

The warrior is typically a well rounded powerhouse. Often sporting a powerful weapon to compliment him. This hero type is a very balance hero. Two common build types for this hero are the god and the guardian.

The god type is often a being who represents some aspect in which he holds order over. This can either be an element/energy type or an abstract concept like life and death.

Example Stats:

Warrior God

Description: (Describe how your character looks)

Strength - 45

Fighting - 12

Agility - 9

Accuracy - 9

Health - 500

Powers:

Lift - 46.7k tons

Heal - d4

Flight - 1,000 mps

Feat; Breath Water

P/T - 60

R- 4 (E, P) 2 (M)

Weapons:

King's Trident (d8)

-Blast (Water, Energy, Wind) d20 + d12 + d4 + 15 (up to 4 targets) and Control

-Energy Shield

-Magic Healing - d12 (up to 4 targets)

-Feat; Return on command

The targets allowed for the blast power of the weapon also applies to the energy/elemental control power. For example, if you pull water from an outside source to attack, you can only target up to 4 targets (refer with GM). The energy stat for the blast power of the weapon also applies to how powerful the energy shield is.

The guardian type differs from the god type in that the guardian usually guards over something like a place, a land, a people or a power source. Sometimes the guardian's powers will reflect what he guards over such as a power source or maybe an animal species in which he watches over.

Example Stats:
Warrior Guardian
Description: (Describe how your character looks)
Strength - 24
Fighting - 16
Agility - 10
Accuracy - 13
Health - 240

Powers:
Lift - 41.1 tons
Heal - d4
P/T - 60
R- 2 (E, P)

Weapons:
Panther Claw (d6) (Gauntlet)
-Enhanced Sense
-Invisibility - 6 ranks
-Teleport - 100 ft

-Luck

Brick

The brick is a very powerful hero in terms of strength and durability. This type of hero often has a monstrous appearance or simply is very large in stature with vast muscles. Often either a solo character or the strong guy of a team, the brick is the type of hero who absorbs a lot of damage and stays in the fight. Usually the brick is a simple hero with only physical stats but may occasionally have a utility power. Two common build types for the brick are the altered form and the powerhouse.

The altered form type is as it sounds. You have a basic or human form and you transform into your superhuman form. Some examples would be steel skin, rock skin, beastly/monster form, etc. The altered form type will sometimes share stats from its basic form and altered form but often will be a lot weaker in regards to stats like strength and health.

Example Stats:
Altered Form
Description: (Describe how your character looks)
Strength - 2/26
Fighting - 8
Agility - 5
Accuracy - 6
Health - 18/210

Powers:
Metal Form (transformation)
-Lift - 50 tons
-Heal - d4
-P/T - 30
-R - 3 (E, P)

*The divided stats in the stats section reflect the non altered form vs the altered form. Refer to the Misc section of the Powers chapter in the core book. All the powers under the transformation form are directly linked to that transformation. When the character is not in their altered form, they do not benefit from the powers connected to that form.

The powerhouse type can be a bulky human or even monstrous/beast like in appearance but does not change form and is simply the most common brick.

Example Stats:
Powerhouse
Description: (Describe how your character looks)
Strength - 32
Fighting - 6
Agility - 4
Accuracy - 5
Health - 250

Powers:
Lift - 75 tons
Heal - d12
P/T - Immune
R - 2 (E, P)

Blaster

The blaster hero is just as it sounds. A hero who's powers focus on some sort of energy creation or manipulation. Though some heroes may have energy powers in their lineup, the blaster's powers are primarily and sometimes only his energy powers. This hero type has many different builds but two common ones are the glass cannon and energy manipulator.

The glass cannon type could be considered street level based on how powerful he is as a whole. This hero can have a blast power ranging from pretty weak to very powerful, but will have very low durability. Though the glass cannon may not have much variety in his abilities, he sometimes will have varying forms of his blast like weaker blast that can target multiple targets, stronger single target blast, and even some blast that create explosions, set people on fire or freeze them. This hero type is often found on teams where he does not need to worry about his shortcomings as much.

Example Stats:
Glass Cannon
Description: (Describe how your character looks)
Strength - 2
Fighting - 3
Agility - 9
Accuracy - 12
Energy - d20 + d8 + 10
Health - 20

Powers:
Blast (Energy)
Wide Blast (Energy) - d20 + 5 (up to 3 targets)
Heal - 1
R - 2 (E)

With the glass cannon type it is good to have a multi target blast in the arsenal but note that it is much cheaper to have the multi target blast a power level or two lower than your normal energy stat to save on points.

The energy manipulator type usually has vast control of a single or multiple energy/elemental type. This type of hero can be very powerful as he does not just have the ability to cause destruction, but to alter his environment. This build will often be well rounded having full energy manipulation (blast and control) over an energy/elemental type as well as the ability to generate energy shields and resistance to the energy/element type he controls. In addition, this hero will often have a travel power like flight or teleport and is also able to take a few hits unlike his glass cannon counter build.

Example Stats:
Energy Manipulator
Description: (Describe how your character looks)
Strength - 2
Fighting - 3
Agility - 7
Accuracy - 13
Energy - d20 + d12 + d4 + 15
Health - 95

Powers:
Blast (Electricity, Force Energy) and Control
Multi Blast (Electricity, Force Energy) - d20 + 5 (up to 5 targets)
Energy Shield
Flight - 770 mph
Heal - d4
R - 5 (Electricity)

Armor Suit

The armor suit type is the story of the normal human trying to hang with superpowered beings. Though this hero can be quite powerful or even resourceful, they are ultimately still a human in a suit and therefore vulnerable when not using their armor. This type can have many different builds but we will focus on three. The universal type which is a general use armor, the agile type which is often light weight and design to be agile and the powerhouse type which focuses on physical strength and durability.

Note that if you add healing to your suit, it will heal the suit and not the person underneath.

The universal armor is design to be able to handle any general situation. It is not for specific use, usually sporting a well balanced set of abilities. The universal armor hero will often have a bit more in the direction of ranged combat over using melee. This type of armor will also usually have flight built in for good measure and is capable of withstanding a lot of damage.

Example Stats:
Universal Armor
Description: (Describe how your character looks)
Strength - 2/12
Fighting - 4
Agility - 6
Accuracy - 6/10
Health - 18/130

Weapons:
Armor (suit)
-Lift - 3.3 tons
-Flight Jet Boots - 500 mph
-(Helmet) Enhance Senses. Feat; Computer Feed

-Palm Blast (Energy) - d20 + 5
-P/T - Immune
-R - 3 (E, P)

Feel free to request customized basic weapons from the GM to be equipped to your suit for free or at a low cost. Such weapons could be a multi targeting bomb/missile launcher built-in in which you would need to restock ammo after running out. The benefit is you would have a weapon for handling groups but since it has a limited amount of ammo (and not based off your base energy stat), you would pay for it with money or in-game resources rather than power points used to build your character.

The suit comes with an energy stat in the form of the palm blast. Any additional basic weapon attached that has a limited amount of ammo does not count as the energy stat when measuring or defining if the suit has an energy stat. If basic weapons (like guns or missile) are attached to the suit and there are no energy stats attach to the suit, the weapons do not count as an energy stat because the suit does not generate energy (for the purpose of using an energy source to power other moves or items you may acquire later on).

The agile suit is just as it sounds, built to be agile and often stealthy. On the low-end this armor provides slightly boosted agility and a small amount of durability. On the higher end the agile suit provides a significant increase of agility (over a normal man) and such built-in abilities like invisibility. Though this type of suit can have flight as a travel ability, it is a more stealthy approach to have something like synthetic webbing or jumping ability.

Example Stats:
Agile Armor
Description: (Describe how your character looks)
Strength - 2/10

Fighting - 8
Agility - 6/15
Accuracy - 6/10
Health - 18/70

Weapons:
Armor (suit)
-Lift - 1.5 tons
-Leap - 25 feet
-Feat; Wall Climb (Hands and Feet)
-(Helmet) Radar Sense (+2 def). Enhance Senses. Feat; Computer Feed
-Web Shooters (Hands)
-Stealth (Invisible) - 3 Ranks
-P/T - Immune
-R - 1 (E, P)

A nice addition to this build as far as adding basic weapon add-ons would be poison darts because they are silent, stealth is the main strength of the agile armor. Be mindful also that your webbing is non-organic so you will have a limited amount in the field.

The powerhouse suit archetype is built to focus on physical strength, melee combat and absorbing a lot of damage. On the lower-end this suit will simply have enhanced physical stats. On the higher-end, this suit will incorporate a shield system which greatly reduces the damage it takes in battle allowing the powerhouse suit to battle with much stronger beings.

Example Stats:
Powerhouse Armor
Description: (Describe how your character looks)
Strength - 2/22
Fighting - 8

Agility - 6
Accuracy - 6/10
Health - 18/180

Weapons:
Armor (suit)
-Lift - 32.2 tons
-Flight Jet Boots - 250 mph
-(Helmet) Enhance Senses. Feat; Computer Feed
-Energy Shield (Energy) - d20
-P/T - Immune
-R - 3 (E, P)

The suit has an energy stat with the chosen power of an energy shield over an energy blast. This is reflected in that you only use the dice portion of the stat for energy shields. If an item was acquired that allowed for a blast power but did not supply the energy stat, this suit would have an attack power of d20 + 5.

Magic User

When you enter the realm of the unexplainable, you enter the magic user. The magic user derives his powers from magic. He often has a wide range of powers he can use connected to his skill in magic which can be expressed in the form of various energy/elemental blast, mental abilities (through the studies of opening one's mind to the mystic arts), protective auras, etc. Depending on the individual magic user, there is nothing they cannot do. The magic user can have all sorts of build types but three general categories are the sorcerer type, occult detective type and the sage type.

With the magic user, whether you use items or innate abilities, you want your hero to have a variety of abilities. For this reason the magic user will focus on having a high energy stat and with multiple forms of energy and energy control. This will allow the magic user to simulate having spells of various types like ice, fire, earth, water, etc, and the ability to form shapes with such elements like weapons, barriers, bridges, etc. You can also have such abilities thru items that give you such powers and control over various energy/elemental types. As a base ability or a starting point the magic user can start with the energy type of magic and with the energy control ability for magic can form objects with the magic such as weapons. And later obtain an item that may add to that magic user's abilities such as to control other various energy/elements.

Another primary ability for a skilled magic user is having a mental stat and telepathy along with mental mind attacks. This would allow a magic user to enter a realm of the mind (or astral realm) and commune with other beings on the non physical plain along with attack and defend against others when not in their presence. (Refer to GM on how this would work and play out in their game)

The sorcerer is a general term magic user which can have any type of focus. This can span from a weak magic user to a powerful magic user.

49

The sorcerer generally has an equal mix of natural magic abilities and magic thru items. Though the items usually give the sorcerer much more variety in the abilities he can do, he can still hold his own with his natural abilities. Some sorcerers, without their magic items, tend to be more or less straight energy blasters with the energy type being magic blast. Another type of sorcerer is the necromancer who focuses in resurrecting the dead and death magic.

Example Stats:
Sorcerer
Description: (Describe how your character looks)
Strength - 1
Fighting - 3
Agility - 6
Accuracy - 12
Energy - d20 + d8 + 10
Mental - 13
Health - 20/150

Powers:
Magic Aura Armor (Transformation)
-P/T - Immune
-Heal - d4
Magic Blast
Energy Shield
Mind Blast
Mind Shield
Telepathy
Flight - 120 mph
R - 2 (M)

Weapons:
Cloak of Invisibility - 6 ranks

Pendant of Time - Time Manipulation

The sorcerer can be built in many different ways. A good option is trying to make him well rounded. If you want to give your sorcerer the ability to "do anything" at a cheap cost (without paying for many different powers), you can use the reality manipulation power. Keep in mind reality manipulation would only apply to powers that activate at that given moment and not for powers requiring constant use.

The boost in health is a reflection of the magic aura armor in the form of a transformation. Refer to the core book under Powers; Misc, for rules on transformation.

Example Stats:
Sorcerer (Necromancer)
Description: (Describe how your character looks)
Strength - 2
Fighting - 3
Agility - 5
Accuracy - 10
Health - 45

Powers:
Heal - d4
Energy Drain - d20 + d8
Magic Healing - d12 (up to 3 targets)
Resurrection - 60% (up to 3 targets) Ranged with zombie control

Weapons:
Staff of Dark Demise (d8) - Dark Energy Blast d20 + d8 + 10
Ring of the Vanish - Teleportation 1,000 ft (up to 3 additional targets)

The necromancer focuses on having a few zombies around him at all times to help protect him or creating a few in the mist of battle. The best tactics for the necromancer is to try to stay in the background and keep resurrecting the dead and healing them. The necromancer is also decently capable of going 1 on 1 if need be by using his energy drain abilities which will keep him in the fight. Items that provide an actual physical or energy based attack is important because health drain cannot actually effect objects like knocking a door down and things of the such.

The occult detective is a very unassuming magic user. A mix of a detective and magic user, they focus on solving the mysteries of the dark underworld. The occult detective generally has more magic thru items than he does natural magic abilities. The magical items he possesses can place him at a very powerful level but generally speaking, without his items, he is not very powerful.

Example Stats:
Occult Detective
Description: (Describe how your character looks)
Strength - 2
Fighting - 9
Agility - 7
Accuracy - 12
Health - 20

Powers:
Feat; Detect Magic, Demons and Dark Energy
Heal - 1

Weapons:
Trench Coat - R - 5 (Dark Energy and Magic Energy)
Revealing Cross (1 ft long)
-Feat; Light (100 ft radius)

-Magic Blast - d12 (up to 10 targets)
-True Sight
Ring of Well-Being
-Plus 100 health
-Heal - d4
Pendant of the Hunter - Enhanced Senses

The Ring of Well-Being adds 100 health to the user making the new total health 120. The ring provides a heal level of d4 which overrides the users heal level if the user has a lower level healing. The healing does not stack with original healing.

The sage is more of a general term of magic user to describe a very powerful and often ancient magic user. This type of user can come in a form of a god or some sort of powerful cosmic entity. The sage generally has a lot of natural magic ability versus using magical items. This type may occasionally have one very powerful magical item to compliment him but often is not dependent on this item to be powerful.

Example Stats:
Sage
Description: (Describe how your character looks)
Strength - 17
Fighting - 6
Agility - 6
Accuracy - 12
Energy - 2d20 + d4 + 20
Mental - 28
Health - 460

Powers:
Lift - 10 tons
Heal - d4

Blast (Fire, Earth, Water, Wind)
Energy/Elemental Control (Fire, Earth, Water, Wind)
Energy Shield
Mind Blast
Mind Shield
Telepathy
Flight - 500 mph
Teleportation - 10,000 miles (up to 4 additional targets)
P/T - Immune
R- 3 (E, P, M)

Weapons:
Third Eye of All Sight (pendant)
-Super Sense (Sight only)
-X-ray Vision
-True Sight
-Precognition (2 ranks)

Robotic

Not every hero is of flesh and blood. The robotic type is a being who is either entirely a machine or partially a machine. Whether his cause is to right the wrongs he has done because of his creator or to discover who he is and his purpose in this world, the robotic type operates completely different from your typical hero. The Robotic hero is less vulnerable to your standard things while more vulnerable to other things. Two very common builds for the robotic type is the robot and the cyborg.

Treat EMP devices as tranquilizer for this type of hero. A virus works the same way poison does for this type of hero. Mental mind attacks do not affect the robot type (but can hurt the cyborg). Robots cannot have mental abilities. The healing power is treated as an auto repair system. First aid comes in the form of a repair kit which functions in the same manner as basic first aid listed in the equipment section. The robotic type can have energy/magic healing in the form of a repair ability for robots only, so somebody choosing this power must state if it is for humans or robotics (which can be used on all mechanical devices). Though robotic types can have an energy healing power for humans (in the form of medical healing), they then cannot use it on themselves.

The robot type is just that, a robot. It has an A.I. system and a built in power source. The robot type can vary from being very standard and weak all the way up to an advance and powerful robot. Often the robot hero will be equipped with various armament from offensive to defensive weaponry.

Example Stats:
Robot
Description: (Describe how your character looks)
Strength - 14
Fighting - 9
Agility - 7

Accuracy - 15
Health - 150

Powers:
Lift - 6 tons
Heal - d4
Feat; computer feed.
Enhanced Senses
R- 3 (E, P)

Weapons:
Shoulder Cannon (d20 + 5) (8 rounds)
Arm Machine Gun (d12 + d4) (30 rounds)

To save on some points for this build, you can have the robot equipped with various normal weapons which your GM may provide for free or at a low cost. The only drawback is you will have a limit on ammo (vs say you paying for a power like energy blast for your range attacks). Because you most likely will not have a healer designed to heal a robot on the team, make sure to provide some healing abilities and maybe even an energy shield for good measure.

The attached weapons are basic weapon add-ons and not from powers. Shoulder cannon is shooting conventional ammo for such a weapon.

The cyborg type is partially human and partially robot. How much so of either depends on how much of himself he kept human (or was able to save). Either way he is all hero. This build is pretty much the same as the robot except he is vulnerable to mental attacks as well as he can possess them.

Example Stats:

Cyborg

Description: (Describe how your character looks)
Strength - 12
Fighting - 9
Agility - 7
Accuracy - 13
Energy - d20 + 5
Health - 135

Powers:
Lift - 3.3 tons
Shoulder Cannon (energy)
Heal - d4
Feat; Computer Feed
Enhance Senses
R- 3 (E, P)

This build is pretty much no different than the robot type as far as how you will play him. Just be mindful though you are able to be damaged by mental mind attacks so feel free to build up a defense for that if you feel it necessary in your build.

*If attacked by mental mind attacks, it goes against his total health. Unlike the armor suit archetype, there is no man under all the metal so he does not have two separate health stats. In the case of the shoulder cannon, it is a power and uses the energy stat.

Shifter

There are those heroes that can alter their form in some way or another, these heroes are called shifters. Shifters are often not very powerful, though some versions can hold their own in a battle. What shifters tend to excel in is the ability to either blend in or overcome obstacles. Shifters have three primary build types, the shapeshifter, the size shifter, and the stretch type.

The shapeshifter focuses on espionage, stealth and infiltration. The shapeshifter is the best swiss army knife for the mission. Often the shapeshifter avoids the battle entirely (when the mission calls for it). This does not mean the shapeshifter cannot fight. The shapeshifter can use animal forms (or made-up forms) to slightly enhance their physical abilities.

Example Stats:
Shapeshifter
Description: (Describe how your character looks)
Strength - 3
Fighting - 12
Agility - 10
Accuracy - 6
Health - 24

Powers:
Heal - d4
Shape shift - 10 ranks

Shapeshifter does not increase its durability when altering its form. Refer to the GM for enhanced physical stats and abilities when transforming into an animal.

The size shifter seems to have the benefit of getting in and out of tight spaces… or making a space tight. The size shifter is not as good at hiding in plain sight as the shapeshifter but makes up for it in the fact that he can increase his strength with his size. Sometimes the size shifter will occupy the space of the strong guy on a team though his powers are not directly strength.

Example Stats:
Size shifter
Description: Height 6ft, weight 180 lbs.
(Describe how your character looks)
Strength - 2
Fighting - 6
Agility - 6
Accuracy - 5
Health - 90

Powers:
Heal - d4
Growth 4/Shrink 4 - 10 ranks of duration
(Quick reference chart)
G1 - 12 ft and 1,440 lbs
G2 - 24 ft and 5.76 tons
G3 - 48 ft and 46 tons
G4 - 96 ft and 368 tons
S1 - 3ft and 22.5 lbs
S2 - 1.5ft and 2.81 lbs
S3 - 9 inches and 5.6 oz
S4 - 4.5 inches and .70 oz

Last we have the stretch hero. Usually the weakest of the archetypes but can still be pretty crafty. This hero never seems in need of rope or even ranged weapons. This hero often fits well in a street level game. Some stretch heroes may also be quite agile making for a bit more versatile of a hero.

Example Stats:
Stretcher
Description: (Describe how your character looks)
Strength - 2
Fighting - 10
Agility - 15
Accuracy - 8
Health - 40

Powers:
Stretch - 5 ranks
Heal - d4
R - 2 (P)

Speedster

When a hero's power is primarily speed, he is known as the speedster. On the lower end the speedster would easily be considered a street level hero. Just being able to travel a few hundred MPH and not much more physically powerful than a standard guy (if at all), the low level speedster is completely at home on a team. The high-end speedster is not that much more powerful than the low-end speedster, but his incredible levels of speed no longer place him at risk of some basic dangers that a much slower character would have to worry about. The high-end speedster is also very durable (relative to a speedster) and with incredibly fast attacks boosting his offense, he can hold his own as a solo hero.

Example Stats:
Speedster
Description: (Describe how your character looks)
Strength - 2
Fighting - 9
Agility - 13
Accuracy - 7
Health - 80

Powers:
Heal - d4
Run - 1,000 mps
Feat; Run on water, Run up walls
Thousand Punch Attack - Plus 4 strength damage
Super Fast Perception (+2 def)

The primary ability of the speedster besides his travel speed is the fast perception power. This ability is what allows him to see things moving at a fast rate and react to them or the ability to take in massive amounts of information in a blink of the eye. The speedster is not a glass cannon, he is not a cannon at all. But you can add such things like a thousand punch

61

attack in the form of a boosted single damage attack which you will add by paying for extra strength but it will be applied to just the attack and not lifting.

Mentalist

The mentalist is a hero whose weapon is literally their mind. Often not very durable physically, they more than make up for this with their offensive and sometimes defensive abilities (though sometimes they can have great physical stats along with strong mental abilities). This archetype can vary in power greatly from being very basic and weak all the way to incredibly strong. Though there are many different builds for this archetype, they all fall under being a telepath, a telekinetic or both. Here we will focus on each separately and breaking each into two subcategories. For each, telepath and telekinetic, you have a more powerful but less tactical hero (Power Mind) and a less powerful, more skilled hero who may use their powers in close combat to more affectively ensure their victory (Battle Mind).

The telepathic power mind has the ability to cause massive damage without even laying a hand on their target. Though this build is often not capable of defending themself very well, they can make up for this in the fact that they can often attack their enemies thru walls or from a distance before even being noticed. Throw in the added bonus that most telepaths can create illusions (in the mind of others), they can often end a battle before it even starts.

Example Stats:
Telepathic Power Mind
Description: (Describe how your character looks)
Strength - 1
Fighting - 3
Agility - 6
Accuracy - 12
Mental - 28
Health - 20

Powers:

Mind Blast (up to 5 targets)
Mind Shield
Telepathic
Illusions (Mental)
R - 5 (M)

The telepathic battle mind is the opposite to its counterpart. Often not as powerful in their ability to do mental damage, they are a lot more of a fierce fighter on the battle field. Often well trained in hand-to-hand combat, the telepathic battle mind will incorporate psychic melee attacks (like fist and kick strikes that attack the mind no matter where they hit on the body). And being that this build relies on being in the center of the battle, they are often at the peak of human physical abilities which means they are pretty good at taking a hit or avoiding a hit (vs a normal person).

Example Stats:
Telepathic Battle Mind
Description: (Describe how your character looks)
Strength - 2
Fighting - 14
Agility - 12
Accuracy - 10
Mental - 19
Health - 22

Powers:
Mind Punch
Mind Blast
Mind Shield
Telepathic
Heal - 1
R - 4 (M)

Weapons:
Katana Sword (d8)
Body Armor +15 Health
Sticky Gauze x3

With the telepathic battle mind, you may want to play them like a crime fighter archetype. To make up for possibly having low physical stats, you can have equipment and gear to keep your hero in the fight longer.

*When using melee mind attacks, you use your fighting stat added to your attack rolls and you do not add strength to the damage. You just apply your mental stat as damage. Damage is of a mind attack and not physical.

The telekinetic power mind is very similar to the glass cannon blaster archetype. Though their attacks are all physical, they can do a lot of things. Their powers range from moving things with their mind to creating nearly indestructible mental force shields.

Example Stats:
Telekinetic Power Mind
Description: (Describe how your character looks)
Strength - 1
Fighting - 3
Agility - 12
Accuracy - 12
Mental - 28
Health - 20

Powers:
Mental Force Blast (up to 3 targets)
Mental Force Shield
Telekinetic

Flight - 120 mph
R - 1 (M)

     The telekinetic battle mind is pretty much the same build as the telepathic battle mind accept mind attacks are traded for mental force attacks. The main difference vs the telepathic battle mind is this build will be able to use their powers to punch thru walls (breaking them) but will lack the versatility of being able to do both physical attacks (like using your normal fist or a weapon) and also being able to use mind attacks (which penetrate armor, physical damage resistance and energy shields/mental force shield).

Example Stats:
Telekinetic Battle Mind
Description: (Describe how your character looks)
Strength - 2
Fighting - 14
Agility - 12
Accuracy - 10
Mental - 19
Health - 22

Powers:
Mental Force Punch
Mental Force Blast
Mental Force Shield
Telekinetic
Leap - 100 ft
Heal - 1
R - 1 (M)

Weapons:

Body Armor +15 Health
Sticky Gauze x 3

When using melee mental force attacks, you use your fighting stat added to your attack rolls and you do not add strength to the damage. You just apply your mental stat as damage. Damage is physical damage.

HOUSE RULES

This section is meant to add extra dimensions to the game. Though it is not require to use these rules, they will expand things as you get better at playing the game. Some of these rules will change the way a player approaches a situation and can make things more challenging or even more beneficial depending on what's going on at the moment in-game.

Distance and Actions/Turns

Distance can have a large impact on your actions and how long it takes for you to get some place or close the distance between you and your target. Depending on your travel speed, it can take you one action to reach your destination/target or several actions. When you are not in combat, distance is not a significant factor unless you have a limited time to reach where you are trying to get to. In combat however, distance can become a very important factor which could get you killed or even save your life.

When it comes to combat and distance, it is measured by how long it takes your character to reach his mark. So the GM may tell you, "You are 2 actions away from reaching the target" (based on your travel speed). This means if you are expecting to do melee combat with your target, it will take you 2 of your actions to reach them allowing for just 1 attack that turn. In the reverse scenario if you have a ranged weapon and your target is 2 actions away from you, it will take 2 actions for them to get into melee range of you which would mean they only get 1 attack against you that turn. This is important because it creates a threat of somebody having a ranged weapon vs melee combat. Now a man holding a gun at you when you are unarmed and they are several actions away from you may cause you to try to talk your way out of the situation or hand over an item if they are demanding for it as you know you are at a disadvantage.

Group Attacking

Melee group attack limit is 4 characters at a time. No more characters can group attack a single target. This is because there is not enough physical space for the target to be surrounded without it becoming a hinderance to the attackers. Ranged group attacks have no limit but everybody must be in sight of the target. But feel free to give a limit to how many people can be in a ranged group attack if you feel it will benefit the game.

Dual Wielding Guns

Placing rules on dual wielding provides a difference and reason to make a decision on whether to use two guns at the same time or one. Realistically if you shoot with two guns at the same time, your accuracy would suffer. This house rule is to reflect this and make the user consider that sometimes it is not the best option to wield two guns while in other situations, the damage is worth the penalty. When dual wielding small firearms, you receive a minus 5 in attack. When dual wielding large firearms, you receive a minus 10 in attack. When dual wielding firearms, simply double the damage dealt (damage resistance is applied first before doubling the damage). Of course you are also doubling the ammo used. Not all large firearms can be dual wielded depending on how they are designed to be used.

Large Objects as Weapons

Sometimes in the world of superheroes random heavy objects become weapons to use in a fight (cars, lamppost, etc). Under these rules, any object that is oversized will act as a d20 for weapon damage (adding your strength stat or mental stat if you have telekineses to the total damage). No matter how much larger an object maybe, it will all fall under this same amount, the large object amount (d20). Most large objects may tend to be destroyed after one use. Refer to the GM.

GAME TIPS

In this section we clarify certain game rules that may not be fully understood. This section also provides a guide on how to use certain powers or game rules in relation to other rules for a better benefit or a clearer understanding.

What is normal healing for a superhero? Your standard run of the mill superhero that has better that normal human healing, whether you are super powerful or just a bit above street level is reflected with a d4 per turn. Below this is considered just above normal human healing (which human level healing is no rate of healing per turn, but by days) while above this is considered to have a fast healing rate even for a superhero.

How can I purchase fast swimming? Just use the same cost for fast running in place of swimming.

Can I use my telekinesis to manipulate and use weapons? Yes. You would apply your mental stat just as you would with strength when you throw a melee weapon. And just like when you throw a weapon, you will also use accuracy for using telekinesis.

Growth power tells me round down in strength while weapon/item's that give strength and stack tell me to round up. Calculate your strength from growth first and then add the strength from the weapon/item and then round up.

Strength 38 to 39 has a huge gap in lifting ability, how does this affect growth strength? With growth and only between 38 and 39 strength level weight, the hero with growth will be able to lift whatever his actual weight is but will act as a strength 38 for the purpose of damage. If the growth weight surpasses the strength level of 39 in weight, calculate as normal again.

How do I create a laser sword? You simply add fire skin power to the stats of a standard sword (d8). Describe the sword so it is understood the context of what the sword is made of (an energy blade that burns). If you want to add energy based damage to any melee weapon, simply add an alternate form of fire skin (electric, etc) to that weapon and describe how the weapon works and looks.

NOW YOU ARE READY!

Now you are ready to take your game to the next level. With a better understanding on how to create your gaming world and a more clear understanding on the rules, your games will be a lot more richer with detail and fun. And the game tips will help to get your mind thinking on all the many ways you can piece things together.

So enjoy and start creating some amazing worlds!